COUNTRY EXPLORERS

ARGENTINA

Suzanne Paul Dell'Oro

Lerner Publications Company • Minneapolis

Lerner Publications Company
A division of Lerner Publishing Group, Inc.
241 First Avenue North
Minneapolis, MN 55401 U.S.A.

Website address: www.lernerbooks.com

Library of Congress Cataloging-in-Publication Data

Dell'Oro, Suzanne Paul.
    Argentina / by Suzanne Paul Dell'Oro.
        p.   cm. — (Country explorers)
    Includes index.
    ISBN 978–0–8225–9413–0 (lib. bdg. : alk. paper)
    1. Argentina—Juvenile literature. I. Title.
F2808.2.D45 2009
982—dc22   2007037100

Manufactured in the United States of America
5 - 51999 - 49451 - 10/7/2021

Table of Contents

Welcome!

Let's explore Argentina! This big country is on the continent of South America. It has many neighbors. Bolivia, Paraguay, and Brazil all sit to the north. Uruguay and the Atlantic Ocean lie to the east. The ocean also winds around Argentina's southern tip. Chile lies to the west.

Argentina

Tourists visit the Perito Moreno Glacier. It lies in the region of Patagonia in southern Argentina.

BOLIVIA

PARAGUAY

BRAZIL

PACIFIC
OCEAN

ANDES

San Miguel
de Tucumán

IGUAZÚ
FALLS

RIO PARANÁ

RIO SALADO

URUGUAY

ARGENTINA

PAMPA

Buenos
Aires

RIO DEL
PLATA

Mar del Plata

ATLANTIC
OCEAN

RIO COLORADO

RIO NEGRO

ANDES

Bariloche

PATAGONIA

PERITO
MORENO
GLACIER

TIERRA
DEL FUEGO

CHILE

N

	mountains
	plains
	plateau
	Lake District
★	country's capital

MILES

0   300

0   300

KILOMETERS

The Andes are the tallest mountains in North or South America.

Going Up?

Argentina has many different landforms. The Andes mountain range forms the biggest one. It makes a long chain of mountains. The Andes start in the northern part of South America. They reach all the way down to the southern tip of Argentina.

6

The Andes act like an umbrella. They keep rain from the west off the eastern mountain slopes. But one spot, called San Miguel de Tucumán, gets lots of water. The water comes from mountain streams.

¡Hola!

That means "hello" in Spanish. Today we visited Iguazú Falls. I have never seen anything like it! It is really 270 waterfalls. We walked on a bridge to see them up close. All that rushing water made me feel dizzy.

I'll be home soon!

Your Frien
Your Tow
Anywhere

Iguazú Falls, Argentina

7

People and Places

Most Argentines live on the Pampa. The Pampa is one of
Argentina's main land areas. A pampa is a flat plain. Wheat
and corn grow well in the Pampa's rich soil. Cows and sheep
have plenty of grass to eat. Large cities also lie on the Pampa.

A cowboy rounds up
cattle on the Pampa.

Patagonia is another main land area. In Patagonia, the land is dry and rocky. And the weather is cold. Not many people live in Patagonia. Most of the people there raise sheep. They use the sheep for their meat and wool.

Land of Fire

Tierra del Fuego is an island. An island is a piece of land surrounded on all sides by water. Tierra del Fuego lies at the southern tip of Argentina. The island got its name from early explorers. They saw campfires burning on the island. They named the island Tierra del Fuego, or "Land of Fire."

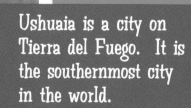

Ushuaia is a city on Tierra del Fuego. It is the southernmost city in the world.

Big City

Buenos Aires is Argentina's biggest city. Can you find Buenos Aires on the map on page 5? More than eleven million people live there. People who live in Buenos Aires are nicknamed *porteños,* or "port people."

The sun sets over the city of Buenos Aires.

Buenos Aires has a busy port. Ships come from around the world. The ships bring machinery to Argentina. They carry away lots of farm products from Argentina.

Pretty in Pink

The president of the United States works and lives in the White House. The White House is in Washington, D.C. The president of Argentina works in a pink building. The building is called Casa Rosada. That means "pink house." Casa Rosada is in Buenos Aires.

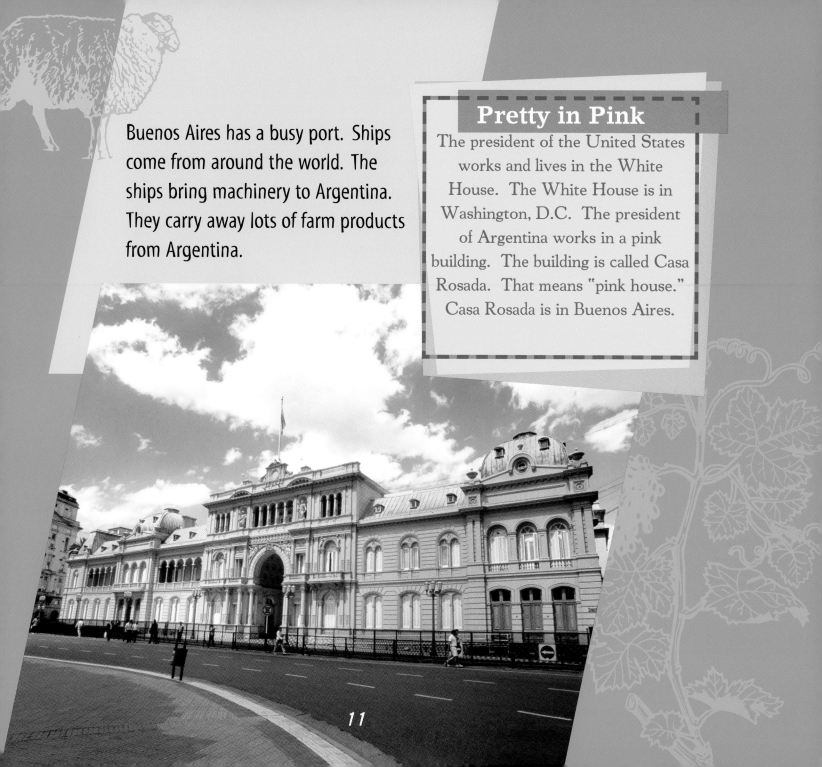

On the Go

Lots of people travel around the cities of Argentina. Streets are often jammed. Many people drive cars. Some people ride a bus. Others take a taxi. The fastest way to get around in some big cities is on an underground train. The train is called a *subte,* or subway.

People board a train in the subway station in Buenos Aires.

In small towns, some people ride horses. Many people walk or pedal bicycles. And others drive cars.

Horses can travel through areas where there are no roads.

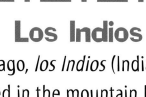

Los Indios

Thousands of years ago, *los Indios* (Indians) lived in Argentina. They lived in the mountain highlands and the plains. Some Indian groups formed communities. They grew crops. Others were hunters and gatherers. They moved from place to place in search of food. Each group had its own language and its own name for itself.

An ancient Indian group used this stone to grind grain into flour.

Cave of Hands

Early Indians left clues about how they lived. Some caves in Argentina have paintings on the walls. The paintings show people dancing or hunting. Other caves show handprints and footprints.

Spanish explorers came to Argentina about five hundred years ago. They fought the native people for land. They killed many Indians. Many others died of sicknesses. Some Spaniards forced native people to work for them as slaves. Other Spaniards married native people. People of mixed Indian and Spanish origins are called mestizos. Only about fifty thousand Indians with no Spanish ancestors live in modern-day Argentina.

Speak to Me

Most people came to Argentina from Spain. Later, many came from Italy. But people from lots of different countries live in Argentina. For example, folks have also come from France, Germany, Great Britain, Poland, Russia, and many other places.

This woman runs a Welsh teahouse in Patagonia. She holds a picture of her great-grandfather. He moved from Wales, in Great Britain, to Argentina.

At home, people may speak the language of their home country. But in schools, stores, and offices, everybody speaks Spanish.

Gypsy Life

The Roma, or Gypsy, is another ethnic group in Argentina. In the past, the Roma usually lived in small groups. They traveled from town to town. And they usually stayed away from other people. The Roma went to town only to buy food or to sell goods. In modern-day Argentina, only about 5 percent of Roma live that way. They live throughout the country. Most live in cities.

Two Roma girls play songs on accordions. They hope that visitors to Buenos Aires will give them coins.

17

This shop sells magazines and newspapers. Most of them are in the Spanish language.

Español

Español, or Spanish, is the official language of Argentina. In Spanish, some letters have different sounds than in English. For example, the letter *j* sounds like *h*. Say the name Julia (HOO-lee-ah). But the letter *h* has no sound at all. The word *hola* (hello) sounds like OH-lah.

Try saying these words:

good-bye	chau	(CHOW)
glad to meet you	mucho gusto	(MOO-choh GOO-stoh)
yes	sí	(SEE)
no	no	(NOH)
see you later	hasta luego	(AH-stah loo-WAY-goh)

The Spanish alphabet has twenty-nine letters. That's three more than the English alphabet has. In Argentina, the double *l (ll)* makes a *zh* sound, like the *s* in treasure. Say *español.* The *ñ* sounds like NYEH in the first *n* in onion. The double *r (rr)* in *burro* sounds like a stick dragged along a picket fence.

ESTE LUGAR NO ES UN HOSPITAL... PERO LA IMPORTANCIA DEL SILENCIO ES LA MISMA. GRACIAS!

This sign asks visitors to be quiet while visiting a national park.

19

An Argentine family walks through La Boca neighborhood in Buenos Aires.

La Familia

La familia is Spanish for "the family." Families are important in Argentina. Most Argentine families are made up of a mother, a father, and children. Grandparents, aunts, and uncles may live in the same house too. Many children also have godparents. Godparents could be family members or close friends. They care about their godchildren. They might go to their godchildren's sports events. They may give them holiday gifts. Sometimes they are just there to talk.

All in the Family

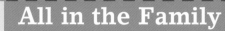

Here are the Spanish names for family members.

grandfather	abuelo	(ah-BWAY-loh)
grandmother	abuela	(ah-BWAY-lah)
father	padre	(PAH-dray)
mother	madre	(MAH-dray)
uncle	tío	(TEE-oh)
aunt	tía	(TEE-ah)
son	hijo	(EE-hoh)
daughter	hija	(EE-hah)
brother	hermano	(her-MAH-noh)
sister	hermana	(her-MAH-nah)

A boy stands with his grandparents at their home in La Rioja.

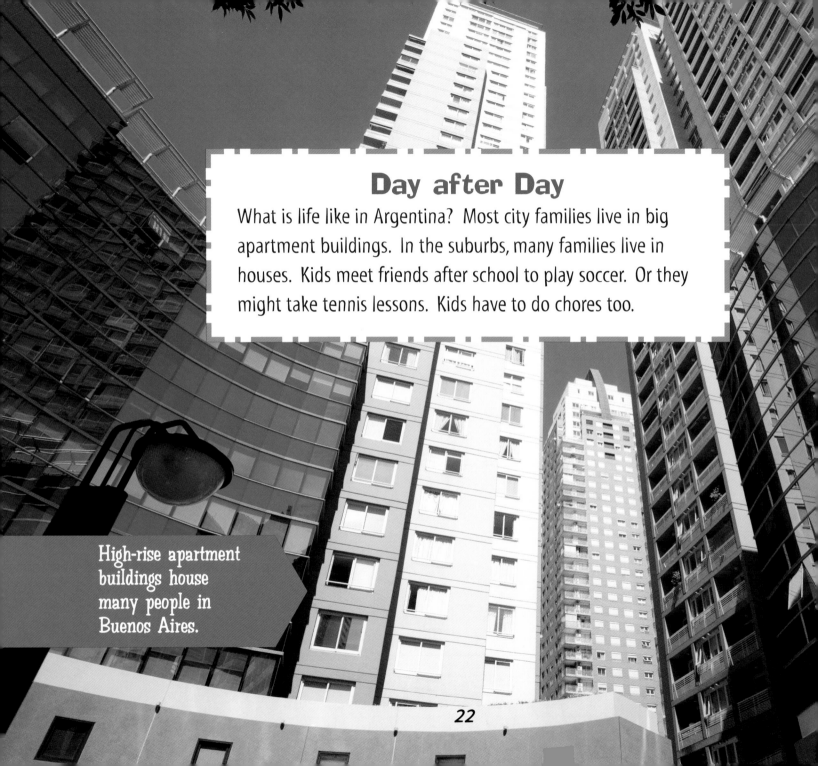

Day after Day

What is life like in Argentina? Most city families live in big apartment buildings. In the suburbs, many families live in houses. Kids meet friends after school to play soccer. Or they might take tennis lessons. Kids have to do chores too.

High-rise apartment buildings house many people in Buenos Aires.

Many country families live on ranches. Kids spend much of their time outdoors. They learn to ride horses. They help grow crops. And they tend farm animals.

Tourists take siesta on a shady porch.

School

Rrrrring! There goes the school bell. Preschoolers line up in the schoolyard. They put their hands on the hips of the child in front of them. Then they march into school in a line.

These children attend a small primary school in central Argentina.

Inside, the kids put on their *guardapolvos.* Those are aprons. The guardapolvos help to keep their clothes clean.

Two schoolgirls wear guardapolvos to school.

A Geography Lesson

Argentine kids go to school while you are on summer vacation. Why? Argentina is in the Southern Hemisphere. The country lies south of the equator. The equator is an imaginary line around the middle of Earth. The equator divides the northern half of Earth from the southern half. In the Southern Hemisphere, the seasons are opposite the ones in the Northern Hemisphere. When it is summer in the United States, it is winter in Argentina.

Lionel Messi (*left*) defends the ball from a Spanish player.

Sports

What is the number one sport in Argentina? ¡Fútbol! *Fútbol* is the Spanish word for soccer. Games appear on television. Local soccer players use neighborhood parks. Argentina's Diego Maradona is one of the world's most famous soccer players. He's no longer playing. But young Lionel Messi is also showing star power.

Tennis, skiing, car racing, field hockey, fishing, and boxing are also popular sports in Argentina.

Playing with Horses

Horses play a big part in Argentina's history. They are still used for travel, especially on the Pampa. *Pato* is a popular game played on horseback. Argentine Indians probably played a version of pato. Two teams of riders pass a ball the size of a soccer ball. A basket stands at each end of the field. A team scores when a player gets the ball through the basket.

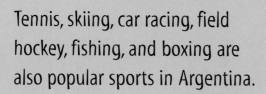

Players compete in the pato championship in Buenos Aires.

City kids climb and slide at a playground. They live in Buenos Aires.

Taking It Easy

Kids everywhere like to have fun, right? In Argentina, they ride bikes. They watch favorite TV shows. Or kids might build a go-cart. During the summer, kids splash in a local swimming pool or at a beach. Many kids meet friends for a soccer game.

Other kids like to roller-skate. In the country, they horse around—on horses.

A girl rides a horse in San Javier Cordoba province.

29

Many people spend their vacations on the beach at Mar del Plata.

Take a Trip

Argentines like to take trips. Argentina has lots of great places to go. Some people visit family members. Other travelers head for the ocean. City folks have picnics in the country. And ranchers sometimes enjoy a day in the city.

The city of Bariloche [bah-ree-LOH-chay] sits in the Lake District of Patagonia. Nahuel Huapi National Park frames the city. Mountains, lakes, and the Río Negro make Bariloche a beautiful vacation spot. Many buildings look as if they could be in a town in Germany.

Check the Time

A tall clock tower stands in Bariloche's main plaza. The clock rings twice every day. Four wooden statues come out of the clock tower. They turn as the clock rings.

Ride 'Em, Cowboy!

An Argentine cowboy is called a gaucho. Years ago, gauchos worked on the Pampa. They watched over herds of cattle. And they lived off the land. True gauchos do not exist anymore.

Gauchos wore shirts, neckerchiefs, and baggy cotton pants called *bombachas*. The outfit was comfortable for long days on a horse.

But Argentines still hold parades and rodeos. A rodeo includes contests on horseback. The events remind people of the old gaucho lifestyle.

Tea Time

Gauchos drank a tea called mate [MAH-tay]. Argentines drink it almost every day. They make it from dried herbs. And they use a special cup to drink it. Argentines use a *bombilla* [bom-BEE-zha] to sip the tea. A bombilla is a metal straw. The straw has a bulb at the end of it. The bulb catches the tea leaves. Friends often share one cup.

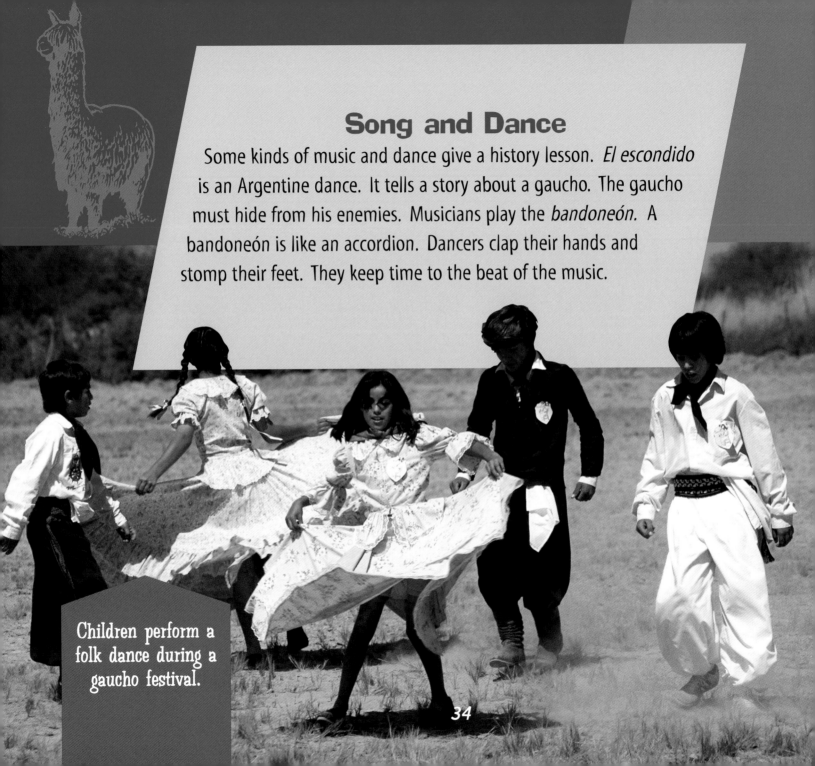

Song and Dance

Some kinds of music and dance give a history lesson. *El escondido* is an Argentine dance. It tells a story about a gaucho. The gaucho must hide from his enemies. Musicians play the *bandoneón*. A bandoneón is like an accordion. Dancers clap their hands and stomp their feet. They keep time to the beat of the music.

Children perform a folk dance during a gaucho festival.

Dance with Me

A famous dance called the tango comes from Argentina. Tango dancers learn hard steps. The tango also has special hand movements. And the dance has its own music. Tango music is often played on the bandoneón.

Professional tango dancers perform at an outdoor café.

Apartment homes in La Boca come in a rainbow of colors.

Picture Perfect

Where can you find art in Argentina? Try La Boca neighborhood of Buenos Aires. Many artists live there. The artists have covered the buildings in this area with bright colors.

The wall paintings, called murals, in El Caminito are huge. El Caminito is a street in La Boca. People walk down the street. But no cars can fit on El Caminito.

Gaucho Artist

Florencio Molina Campos was born in Buenos Aires in 1891. He painted pictures of gaucho life on the pampa. His style looked like cartoons. For a short time, he worked with filmmaker Walt Disney in Hollywood, California. Molina Campos died in 1959.

Schoolchildren look at a mural in El Caminito.

Grill It!

Beef is the most popular food in Argentina. Argentines like to grill beef over an open fire. They also grill other meats, as well as fish, chicken, and turkey.

Cooks don't need a big fire to grill meat. This man uses a small grill over a few hot coals to make his dinner.

Shoppers order fresh beef at a butcher shop in Buenos Aires.

Supermarkets are popping up in Argentine cities. But not long ago, there were none. Most Argentines shopped at smaller markets for fresh fruit and vegetables. They went to butcher shops to buy fresh meat. And bakeries sold fresh bread. One kind of store, called a *galletitería,* sells only crackers and cookies.

Holy Days

Most Argentines belong to the Roman Catholic Church. Many towns even have their own saint (holy person). Townspeople do something special to honor their saint every year.

Basílica de Nuestra Señora del Pilar is one of the oldest churches in Buenos Aires. Catholics built it in 1732.

Christmas is also an important religious holiday. Instead of Santa Claus, Papá Noel brings gifts. But children really look forward to Three Kings Day. That happens on January 6. Christians believe three kings gave gifts to the baby Jesus on this day. Children leave their shoes outside the door. They believe the kings will fill them with gifts.

A statue of Papá Noel welcomes shoppers to a mall in Buenos Aires.

Celebrate!

Argentines also honor their country. And they honor their culture. Vendimia is the grape festival. People praise the rich earth. The earth helps the grapes to grow. Argentines hold a snow festival in Bariloche. They honor the snowy mountains there. Argentines also honor the sea. They do this in the first week of December. The townspeople of Mar del Plata have a party during the National Sea Festival.

A grape grower cuts ripe grapes in a vineyard. Growers brought the seeds of these grapes from France more than a hundred years ago.

Let's Dance

The tango is danced in countries all over the world. But the Argentines hold their own tango festival. An international festival happens in Buenos Aires in late February and early March. Music and dancers flood the streets during this festive celebration of Argentine culture.

Couples perform in a tango festival championship.

THE FLAG OF ARGENTINA

Argentina's flag has one white stripe between two light blue stripes. Blue and white are the colors of Argentine patriots. The patriots fought off British invaders in 1806 and 1807. In the center of the white stripe is an image of a sun. The sun stands for Argentina's freedom from Spain in 1816.

FAST FACTS

FULL COUNTRY NAME: República Argentina (Argentine Republic)

AREA: 1,073,512 square miles (2,780,400 square kilometers), or as big as the states of Arizona, California, Colorado, Nevada, New Mexico, Oklahoma, Texas, and Utah put together

MAIN LANDFORMS: Mountain range: Andes. Island: Tierra del Fuego. Plains: the Pampas. Plateau: Patagonia

MAJOR RIVERS: Colorado, Negro, Paraná, de la Plata, Salado

ANIMALS AND THEIR HABITATS: mountain lions (mountains); peccaries, monkeys, jaguars, marsupials, porcupines, chinchillas, deer, and pumas (forests); guanacos, armadillos, wild horses, alpacas, foxes, llamas, and hares (grasslands); tapirs (lowlands); swamp deer and capybaras (marshes); lizards, otters (rivers); dolphins, sea lions, and whales (ocean); penguins (ice fields)

CAPITAL CITY: Buenos Aires

OFFICIAL LANGUAGE: Spanish

POPULATION: about 40,301,927

GLOSSARY

continent: any one of Earth's seven large areas of land. The continents are Africa, Antarctica, Asia, Australia, Europe, North America, and South America.

equator: an imaginary line that circles Earth at the middle, dividing the world into a northern half and a southern half

gaucho: an Argentine cowboy

grill: a way of cooking meat or fish over an open flame or on hot coals

landform: a natural feature, such as a mountain or a plain

mountain range: a series, or group, of mountains—the parts of Earth's surface that rise high into the sky

mural: a large-scale work of art painted on a wall

Northern Hemisphere: the half of Earth's surface that lies above the equator

pampa: a large area of flatland covered by grass

plaza: a public square in a city or town

port: an area on the shore of a body of water where ships can load and unload goods safely

rodeo: a contest with some events performed on horseback. Rodeo events include calf roping and bull riding.

Southern Hemisphere: the half of Earth's surface that lies below the equator. Argentina is in the Southern Hemisphere.

subway: an underground train that moves large numbers of people quickly

TO LEARN MORE

BOOKS

Brusca, María Cristina. *My Mama's Little Ranch on the Pampas.* New York: Henry Holt, 1994. Maria tells about her first year on her mother's ranch in Argentina.

Kalnay, Francis. *Chúcaro: Wild Pony of the Pampa.* New York: Harcourt Brace, 1993. This Newbery Medal Honor Book presents the adventures of a boy and his pony on the Argentine Pampa.

Van Laan, Nancy. *The Magic Bean Tree: A Legend from Argentina.* Boston: Houghton Mifflin, 1998. This legend tells about a boy who saves the creatures of the Pampa.

WEBSITES

Argentine Children's Songs
http://www.mamalisa.com/world/argentin.html
Listen to songs that kids sing in Argentina and sing along yourself with lyrics in English and Spanish.

Time for Kids/Go Places: Argentina
http://www.timeforkids.com/TFK/goplaces/main/0,18606,491291,00.html
Explore Argentina's most amazing places, check out Argentina's history, and even send an e-card to a friend.

INDEX